W9-AMC-720

Peerless

by Jiehae Park

‖ SAMUEL FRENCH ‖

FOR PRODUCTION INQUIRIES
UNITED STATES AND CANADA
info@concordtheatricals.com
1-866-979-0447

UNITED KINGDOM AND EUROPE
licensing@concordtheatricals.co.uk
020-7054-7298

Each title is subject to availability from Concord Theatricals Corp.,
depending upon country of performance. Please be aware that
PEERLESS may not be licensed by Concord Theatricals Corp. in your
territory. Professional and amateur producers should contact the
nearest Concord Theatricals Corp. office or licensing partner to verify
availability.

No one shall make any changes in this title(s) for the purpose of production. No part of this book may be reproduced, stored in a retrieval system, scanned, uploaded, or transmitted in any form, by any means, now known or yet to be invented, including mechanical, electronic, digital, photocopying, recording, videotaping, or otherwise, without the prior written permission of the publisher. No one shall share this title(s), or any part of this title(s), through any social media or file hosting websites.

For all inquiries regarding motion picture, television, online/digital and other media rights, please contact Concord Theatricals Corp.

MUSIC AND THIRD-PARTY MATERIALS USE NOTE

Licensees are solely responsible for obtaining formal written permission from copyright owners to use copyrighted music and/or other copyrighted third-party materials (e.g., artworks, logos) in the performance of this play and are strongly cautioned to do so. If no such permission is obtained by the licensee, then the licensee must use only original music and materials that the licensee owns and controls. Licensees are solely responsible and liable for clearances of all third-party copyrighted materials, including without limitation music, and shall indemnify the copyright owners of the play(s) and their licensing agent, Concord Theatricals Corp., against any costs, expenses, losses and liabilities arising from the use of such copyrighted third-party materials by licensees. For music, please contact the appropriate music licensing authority in your territory for the rights to any incidental music.

IMPORTANT BILLING AND CREDIT REQUIREMENTS

If you have obtained performance rights to this title, please refer to your licensing agreement for important billing and credit requirements.

PEERLESS was first produced by the Cherry Lane Mentor Project (Producing Artistic Director, Stephanie Ybarra; Associate Producer, Michael Bulger; Founding Artistic Director, Angelina Fiordilisi) at Cherry Lane Theatre's Studio Theatre from March 4-14, 2015. The performance was directed by Margot Bordelon, with scenic design by Edward T. Morris, costume design by Moria Sine Clinton, lighting design by Oliver Wason, and sound design by composer Palmer Hefferan. The production stage manager was Anne Huston. The cast was as follows:

M	Tiffany Villarin
L	Teresa Avia Lim
BF	Christopher Livingston
D / D'S BROTHER	Gideon Glick
DIRTY GIRL / PREPPY GIRL	Emma Ramos

PEERLESS had its world premiere subsequently produced for Yale Repertory Theatre (Artistic Director, James Bundy; Managing Director, Victoria Nolan) from November 27 – December 19, 2015. The performance was directed by Margot Bordelon, with scenic design by Christopher Thompson, costume design by Sydney Gallas, lighting design by Oliver Wason, and sound design and original music by Sinan Refik Zafar. The production stage manager was Victoria Whooper. The cast was as follows:

M	Tiffany Villarin
L	Teresa Avia Lim
BF	Christopher Livingston
D / D'S BROTHER	JD Taylor
DIRTY GIRL / PREPPY GIRL	Caroline Neff

The New York premiere of *PEERLESS* was produced by Primary Stages (Andrew Leynse, Artistic Director; Shane D. Hudson, Executive Director) on October 11, 2022. It was directed by Margot Bordelon, the scenic design was by Kristen Robinson, the costume design was by Amanda Gladu, the lighting design was by Mextly Couzin, the sound design was by Palmer Hefferan, the fight direction was by Michael Rossmy, the props supervision was by Sean Sanford, and the cultural consultation was by Vickie Ramirez. The production stage manager was Megan Schwartz Dickert. The cast was as follows:

M	Sasha Diamond
L	Shannon Tyo
BF	Anthony Cason
D / D'S BROTHER	Benny Wayne Sully
DIRTY GIRL / PREPPY GIRL	Marié Botha

CHARACTERS

M & L – twin sisters, Asian

BF – M's boyfriend, Black

D – male, looks (really) white, Native American

DIRTY GIRL – a.k.a. Caroline a.k.a. That Weird Girl in High School You Know the One, white

D'S BROTHER – (doubles with D)

PREPPY GIRL – (doubles with Dirty Girl)

SETTING

Midwestern suburbia

High school

AUTHOR'S NOTES

Some notes on style, pace, etc:

This play is a comedy. Until it's not.

Words in (parentheses) are spoken, but have less weight than non-parentheticals.

There is a marked difference in the ways the twins speak to adults, their peers, and each other.

But in general: lots of overlaps,* *fast.*

Periods (.) in dialogue, as well as beats, pauses, and silences in stage directions, serve important functions in the rhythm of the text, often (though not always) indicating the end of a build and/or a shift in intention. Please do not skip over them. Conversely, do not add unscripted beats and pauses, as they will undermine the existing structure.

Transitions, like the rest of the play, should be light and quick (or if that's not possible, at least entertaining).

Run time: 75 minutes.

---

*Overlaps are indicated by a "/" – the character with the next line should begin speaking when that symbol appears in the text. For example, in the following sequence, L's "Inform" would be spoken simultaneously with M's "inform." L's "that" would be spoken at the same time as M's "Your."

M."We regret to / inform…"

L. "Inform you… / that"

M. Your spot in this year's upcoming class has been taken

THE STORY

At heart, this play is a love story between two sisters. As in life, people do all kinds of terrible things out of love (or what they convince themselves is love); a big trap here (true also for *Macbeth*) is to play L as a two-dimensional evil schemer – the tragedy is far richer if her actions come out of genuinely wanting to help, but are interpreted by M as selfishly driven.

Additionally, the play flirts with stereotypes in order to subvert them, not to present those stereotypes as two-dimensional truth. Please be cognizant of whether we are asking the audience to laugh "at" or "with" the characters in the play. Approach with love, always – it makes for better theatre.

THE GIRLS

It may be helpful to think of the physical position of the girls in staging as reflective of the evolution of their relationship. When are they side by side, together against the world? When is one turned toward the other but the other not looking? When are they turned directly toward each other in confrontation? When are they completely alone?

HOOPCOMING

In Hoopcoming, it may be fun to see how much of the time D can spend dancing (consciously or unconsciously) – physical movement can really help with building the motor under his speech that is required to propel us through that scene. If the actor playing D doesn't have a lot of breath capacity initially, you may have to work up to it – that scene is a monster.

TRANSITIONS

There is very little time for scenic transitions – the play should always feel like it's falling forward. If you don't have dressers or backstage help, it may be worth simplifying costume elements to facilitate the fluidity of forward motion. If you need to fill transitions with some nonverbal storytelling, go for it (but no words please!).

PACE

Ultimately, the pace of the play should be a little scary to the performers, but not so scary as to prevent listening and responding. Faster than normal but not so rushed as to be thoughtless. Fun-scary, like a rollercoaster rather than a rabid dog.

"We are yet but young indeed."
– Macbeth

1. Mail

(A heavy, stuffed-to-the-brim, 10x13 envelope falls from the sky. Thud.)

2. Dirty Girl

> (**DIRTY GIRL** *appears. She is a white girl with dreadlocks, wearing a filthy trenchcoat. She hasn't showered in weeks [months?]. She is bent over, talking to something in her pocket.*)

DIRTY GIRL. Shhhh

I said shhhh

I said

Yes

But

Not

Yet.

> (*The sound of squeaking. Small, rodent-like.*)
>
> (*Something scurries across the stage on tiny feet.*)

3. Early Decision

(A school bell.)

(The twins.)

(Matching outfits, except for their nylon backpacks – **M** *red,* **L** *yellow.)*

(They watch someone walk by with bright, frozen smiles. Then drop them.)

L. Did you hear

M. I can't

L. You heard

M. I can't

L. I'm sorry

M. *believe*

L. I know

M. Did you see

L. I know

M. You did

L. I did

M. The *smile*

L. I saw

M. On his

L. fat

M. His *fat*

L. fugly

M. His *fugly* fat

L. Veiny

M. His *veiny* fat

L. Face

M. His veiny fat

L. Hands

M. on his fat fucking envelope. Whereas I.

L. Whereas you

M. Whereas I

L. / You

M. I got *this.*

> *(She drops a crumpled, single piece of paper on the ground.)*

   "We regret to / inform…"

L. "Inform you… / that"

M. your spot in this year's upcoming class has been taken

L. Occupied

M. Seized

L. Usurped

M. *Usurped* by a no-good no-talent no-brain-fat-fuck. How.

L. How?

M. How

L. (well)

M. How did this –

> *(They watch someone walk by.)*

> *(A lightbulb:)*

   Ohmygod his brother.

L. His brother?

M. His *brother*

L. His

M. reason

L. The / reason

M. Of course

L. You think?

M. his retard / brother

L. his / brother is ?

M. *Duh* of / course

L. really?

M. Because of / his

L. you think that's enough to

M. how else

L. well

M. I bet he wrote in / his

L. The essay.

M. His essay

L. What did you

M. Africa

L. Summer?

M. My summer in / Africa

L. That's good

M. It's bullshit. It's *normal* it's *boring* I mean / *you were there*

L. I was there

M. Whereas *he* has

L. You think?

M. A retard

L. I don't

M. Not *my* fault you're not / retarded.

L. I think / maybe

M. It's not like

L. I think he's

M. / *He's* retarded

L. got like *cystic* / fibersis

M. / I mean sure if *he* were overcoming

L. fi*bro*sis

M. you know, *personal retardation*

L. That would be

M. *maybe*

L. That would / be

M. I mean *maybe*

L. Okay

M. I'm a *girl*

L. Yeah

M. *Double* Minority

L. Well I think they're / actually

M. *Double Mi/nority.*

L. they're like thirty percent

M. *Minority vagina.*

L. And we both know it's harder for us / than for

M. *Affirmative action.*

L. It's not like you're *black*

M. *American Dream*

L. Or like *poor*

M. *I know that why are you telling me things I know I wish you were actually as retarded as you sound right now because then I would be going to College.*

L. You're going to go to –

M. *The* College.

L. *("Right.") The College*

M. Trees and

L. Brick

M. Colonial

L. Columns

M. Low teacher to student

L. The Quad

M. The Field

L. The History

M. The Future

L. The *Future*

M. My Future

L. *Our* Future
    You and then

M. You

L. You still could get

M. *One*

L. You still

M. They take *one*
    Every year
    They take *one*

L. They take one
   Historically / but

M. *Early.*

L. Yes.

M. *Early Deci/sion*

L. Maybe this year / they'll

M. *Deferred.*

L. You could still

M. *I'm deferred*

L. You could still get in / Regular

M. I was a shoo-in

L. A sure thing

M. My stats are

L. Impeccable

M. 4.8

L. (weighted)

M. 4.0 *Un*
   1600

L. (second try)

M. *So* (?)

L. (no/thing)

M. Consistently *first*
   He's not even top ten

L. Close

M. No not even

L. Eleven

M. There's no way his stats are

L. Well what about softs?

M. His softs?
   My softs are

L. Killer

M. They're killer
   No way his / softs are

L. No way his

M. Retard or no

L. (I don't think he's / retarded)

M. No contest
   This fucks with *everything*
   Me and then you

L. Could still get in Regular

M. *Fucks* me and then you

L. Could still get in Regular

M. *You know the odds*

L. But you

M. You've seen the data
   The last twenty years
   One they take *one*

L. Still
   Could get in Regular
   or Something Could Happen

M. like what

L. Like that kid

M. Like what kid

L. In 2001
   His mom got like cancer

M. / So

L. So he *deferred*

M. He deferred?

L. He deferred from The College

M. So what did They do

L. They took someone else and he went the next year

M. They took someone Regular?

L. No *right away.*

> *(Beat.)*

M. Can we give his mom cancer?

L. Can't *give* someone cancer

M. Is cancer contagious?

L. Yeah no

M. (yeah I *know*)
But something less serious

L. Jen's cat has Cat AIDS

M. Ohmygod *AIDS*
Can people get Cat AIDS?

L. Well Jen doesn't have it

M. Oh / yeah

L. Wait if he deferred
That would mean that *next year* I'd

M. shit that's right shit
But if I were *in*
you'd get sibling preference

L. It's not that clear cut
If he defers
it's not me *versus* him
It's him a year late
It's him *guaranteed*

M. Shit

L. You and then

M. You
That's what we planned for
Me and then

L. Me

M. That's why we came here

L. That's why I stayed back for

M. All of these years of me

L. And then me

M. Living in

L. Nowheresville

M. All for the sake of

L. Geographical

M. Diversity

L. A shoo-in

M. A promise

L. A promise

M. *They promised*

L. A shoo-in

M. A sure thing

L. A hedging

M. An edge

L. Geographical Diversity

M. Why else would

L. You still could

M. Stop

L. Might get in Regular

M. *Stop.*

L. / I

M. *I said stop.*

L. I.

>   *(Beat.)*

>   Sorry.

>   *(Beat.)*

>   Sorry.

>   *(Silence.)*

>   *(Finally:)*

>   He's Native American.

>   *(Beat.)*

M. What.

L. He's

M. / No

L. yes he's I heard he's

M. From who

L. From whom

M. Fuck you

L. It's a preposition.

M. I *know*

L. "From" is / a –

M. *I know*

L. "whom" is the object of the / preposition so you have to use the object case

M. *I know that you don't think I know "from" is a preposition I have a four-point-eight weighted, four-point-oh un* you *have a four-point-six weighted three-point-nine* un, *you don't think I know that?*

> *(Beat.)*

L. / I heard

M. Fuck you you heard.

L. He's –

M. *Look* at him

L. Technically

M. Fuck

L. His Great Grandma

M. His what?

L. (or his great great)

M. / No

L. So technically

M. Fuck.

L. I guess *technically*

M. / Fuck fuck fuck

L. speaking he's –

> *(Beat.)*

M. Don't say it.

> *(Beat.)*

L. He's

M. Don't

L. He's

M. Don't

L. He's

M. Don't you say don't you fucking say that fucker is
L. One-sixteenth Native American.

>   *(Beat.)*
>   *(**M** screams.)*
>   *(The school bell.)*

4. Detention

*(M and **DIRTY GIRL** at parallel desks.)*

*(**DIRTY GIRL** throws little bits of paper at **M** with each repetition of "hail.")*

DIRTY GIRL. Hail.

M. What

DIRTY GIRL. Hail.

M. Stop

DIRTY GIRL. Hail.

M. Will you *stop* with the

DIRTY GIRL. Hail.

M. It's not hail it's / trash

DIRTY GIRL. Hail.

*(**M** ignores her.)*

That was some scream

*(**M** ignores her.)*

That was some scream you screamed

*(**M** ignores her.)*

Didn't think your mousey mouth could let out a scream like that

*(**M** whips around toward her.)*

M. I thought you didn't talk.

Isn't that your thing? Dirty and dumb?

DIRTY GIRL. I know about you

*(**M** turns back, trying to ignore her.)*

About you and your sister

I know about you

*(**M** still ignores her.)*

About you and your outfits

*(**M** still ignores her.)*

DIRTY GIRL. About you and your kind

> *(That got her.)*

M. "Your kind"?

DIRTY GIRL. I know what you're like
and I *hail* / you.

M. You racist / bitch

DIRTY GIRL. Nerds

M. Oh

DIRTY GIRL. Chinky nerds

> *(**M**'s hand shoots up.)*

M. *(To the front of the room.)* Mr. / Kahl?

DIRTY GIRL. Hail.

M. Dirty Girl won't stop / throwing

DIRTY GIRL. Hail.

M. Fine, *"Caroline"* won't stop / throwing

DIRTY GIRL. Hail.

M. And *"Caroline"* is slinging racial / epithets

> *(**M** strains her hand up farther, accidentally striking a resemblance to an awful historical gesture that **DIRTY GIRL** mocks:)*

DIRTY GIRL. Sieg Heil!

M. and seriously Nazi

DIRTY GIRL. *(Taking out a cigarette.)* All Hail

M. *WILL YOU STOP IT ALREADY*

> *(Without breaking eye contact, **DIRTY GIRL** produces a lighter from nowhere and lights her cigarette.)*
>
> *(She blows smoke in **M**'s face.)*

Are you kidding me.

> *(The school bell.)*
>
> *(**M** stands to go.)*

DIRTY GIRL. *(A whisper.)* I know about you

You and your kind and your plans for *The College.*

>   (**M** *turns back.*)

Why you came here
Invaded
You and then her
How she *stayed back a year*
Dividing to conquer
Plotting and planning
Stealing the Future

M. You're talking like crazy
You're Dirty and Crazy

DIRTY GIRL. But you didn't get in
Awww you didn't get / in

M. Blow / me

DIRTY GIRL. *(Careless.)* But you will
And your little dog too.

M. Whatever

>   (**DIRTY GIRL** *blocks her path.*)

I've gotta get to / Stats

DIRTY GIRL. Stats your stats

M. You're weird

DIRTY. I know things
I know / things

M. Nothing.

>   (**DIRTY GIRL** *looks her in the eye.*)

DIRTY GIRL. Sixteen hundred and four-point-eight weighted four-point-oh *un* with sixteen APs and piano on Sundays since five years old Sundays were always your favorite color is peaches 'n cream and your favorite dessert is peaches 'n cream and your favorite place is peaches 'n cream when Hoopcoming weekend they find him his body the colors of peaches 'n cream he'll have a skinny smile on his fat fat face.

Oh Yeah Also you got a ninety-nine-point-five on your
Stats final. Point-five deduction for meters squared.

M. I got a hundred Dyas loves me I always get a hundred

> *(Beat.)*

Oh Yeah Also you're a crazy racist bitch.

> *(**M** starts to go.)*

> *(**DIRTY GIRL** grabs her arm.)*

DIRTY GIRL. Fat future coming for his fat face.
Winner.
Winner winner chicken dinner.
Hail.
Hail.
Hail.

5. Stats (Class)

*(**M** and **BF** sit in the back of the classroom, holding their Stats finals.)*

M. Point-five deduction

BF. That's good

M. *("Damn.")* Fuck me.

BF. *(Flirting.)* Now?

M. Stop it

BF. Relax.

M. *Point five* deduction

BF. Come 'ere

M. *Point five*

BF. Seriously?

M. (I know) Is he serious?

BF. I meant are you serious?

M. "meters."

BF. It was feet

M. Of course it was feet the whole thing was in feet.

BF. Feet's not meters

M. I *clearly* meant feet

BF. but you didn't / write

M. It's not a *conversion* test

BF. Feet aren't meters

M. It's not a *memory* / test

BF. Why are you getting so / worked

M. Dyas loves me / why would he

BF. Yeah…about that

M. He loves me

BF. That's clear to everyone.

(Beat.)

M. What's that supposed to mean?

BF. Let's talk about something else

M. *What.*

BF. Like what we're doing for Hoopcoming

M. Fuck Hoopcoming
   What did you

BF. Nothing.

M. It didn't sound / like

BF. Relax

M. Don't tell me to

BF. Sorry

M. Don't touch me

BF. It's just that

M. Is just *what*

BF. The flirting

M. What / flirting

BF. It's / gross

M. Gross he's my *teacher*

BF. Yeah and you're practically

M. Gross you're so gross

BF. "Ni hao" he said

M. So

BF. And you said back "ni hao"

M. And

BF. you're not fucking Chinese

M. It's like "Hola" or / "Bonjour"

BF. *(Mumbling.)* s'tryin to be all *down with the ethnics*

M. Oh are we talking "black" now / I didn't know we

BF. Whoa hey now whoa hey

M. There's no *Historically Asian College* I can apply to

BF. It's not about

M. Some of us need all the help we can get

BF. There's help and there's *help*

M. He wrote one of my recs

BF. Well he's always like *standing*

M. he's standing

BF. near*by*

M. Near what?

BF. Near you

M. Well not now

BF. Uh yeah there's a *sub.*

> (**BF** *takes out a Snickers and takes a huge bite.*)

M. You are such a pig.

BF. *(Chewing.)* I'm growing I'm hungry.

> *(He swallows.)*

I know you're upset about

M. Fine

BF. There *are* / other

M. *Fine.*

BF. *(Not at all convincing.)* You could still get in / Regular

M. Fine, I said FINE.

Why is everyone *oppressing* me today?

> (**BF** *takes another bite.*)

BF. Are you mad?

Are you mad at / me?

M. Whatever.

BF. Not whatev / er

M. It's whatever / okay

BF. No it's

> (**M** *stands.*)

M. *(To the sub.)* Mr. Sub?

Mr. Sub?

I have to go to the restroom

My boyfriend and I just broke up and I'm really / upset

BF. What?

M. I'm really upset so / could I

BF. You can't

M. *(To* **BF.***)* I can
   (To the sub.) please thank you
   (To **BF.***)* We're over bye.

6. Voicemail

(L on the phone, warming up for ballet.)

M'S VOICEMAIL. It's me. Leave it.

L. It's me.

    I got your text.

    That's weird.

    That's weird.

    That's so freaking weird

    She's so freaking Dirty and weird but that's *weird.*

    Where are you

    Because listen

    I think

    I think

    I think she may have like

    Magical Powers

    I'm serious

    Seriously

    I'm serious

    I know that sounds

    But I'm Serious

    Because listen

    Gabby

    Gabby

    Gabby told me she sees her one afternoon

    In the parking lot of Lee's apartment complex

    With this RAT

    With this RAT in her HAND

    And she was like

    singing

    and holding it

    like a baby

    A little rat baby

    And when she was done with her rat baby song

She lit a cigarette and walked
Didn't smoke it just lit it
Stuck it flame-up in the dirt
And walked
And that night
That night
Lee's mom's making dinner
Like meatloaf
Or fish
I don't know
Dinner
In her uniform
from work
Her like polyester
like apron
or smock
like a second grader
Anyway
she was making this dinner and her uniform
her apron
caught *fire*
and she threw it off and
the kitchen
caught *fire*
and the whole place filled up
with *fire*
or I guess smoke
it filled up with smoke
and they had to leave
they opened up all of the
doors and the windows to air out the
Anyway
they're back
they come back

and the smoke is gone
and there's no more fire
and no more smoke
and it's cold 'cause all of the doors and the windows
and the kitchen *the kitchen*

(Beat.)

the whole kitchen floor is covered in rats.

(Beat.)

a family of rats
a momma rat
a daddy rat
three baby rats
Dead
Of course dead
So
So
Lee takes out the trash
with their little rat bodies
like inside the bag
But when he gets outside
the bag starts to *move*
To squeak and to move
He could *hear* them he said
squeaking and moving and eating and

(She shudders.)

She did it, Lee thinks
Gabby said that Lee thinks
It was her
Cuz of that thing that he said
It was her
Remember that thing at the pool
'Bout her hair
'Bout her smell

'Bout her dirt
It was *her.*
So
I've been thinking
I thought
I think
She never says anything
never you know?
So those things that she *told you*
those things that she *knew*
about you and me
Maybe she *sees* things
Maybe she *sees* that
Something *Could* Happen
What she said about you and finding his
Finding him
Finding
Well maybe
Just maybe
There's
Something
She
Knows.

Because here's the thing.

I heard about your breakup (he probably deserved it)
The whole school heard (he totally deserved it)
You're like really loud (it's okay though I love you)
Here's the thing.
You'll never guess who asked me after AP Euro if that
meant you needed a Hoopcoming date.

　　　(She pauses. For drama.)

Call me.

　　　(She waits.)

(The sound of an automated recording: "If you're satisfied with your message, press one. If you'd like to re–")

(She hits one and holds it.*)*

(BEEEEEEEEEEEEEEEEEEEEEEEEEEEEEEEP.)

7. Track

(The sound of heavy breathing.)
(Track practice.)
*(**M** running with iPhone.)*
(She finishes her last lap.)
(A voicemail notification.)
(She listens.)

8. Hoopcoming

(Bad pop music.*)*

(Disco-ball-refracted light.)

(Basketball-themed decorations ["Hoopcoming!"].)

*(**D** and **M** stand awkwardly, waiting.)*

*(**D** is not actually overweight. Maybe his hands are a little disproportionately fleshy. But he's a normal-sized kid [maybe, though not necessarily, with bad skin].)*

(A few seconds. Then:)

*(**L** comes back, wiping her neck.)*

*(**M** and **L** are wearing matching semi-formal dresses with different colored hair flowers [**M** red, **L** yellow].)*

D. I'm sorry

L. It's fine

D. Sometimes / he

L. it's fine

D. Is he

L. Bathroom

Yeah I could hear him

Like hacking

D. it's loud

L. Like a lot

It's *scary*

D. At home he's got this um

Vest?

It helps with the mucus

---

*A license to produce *Peerless* does not include a performance license for any third-party or copyrighted music. Licensees should create an original composition or use music in the public domain. For further information, please see the Music and Third-Party Materials Use Note on page iii.

The Vest.
The Vest Is Life
We joke that sometimes

L. And the smell
　is that

D. oh

L. you can smell
　from the hall

D. sometimes he gets gas?
　it's a symptom of

　　　　(Beat.)

He's nervous
It's worse
When he's nervous
Or happy
It's a compliment
Really

　　　　(Beat.)

He may be a while.

　　　*(**L** manages a smile.)*

L. I get it
　I'm flattered
　It's sweet

D. Really?

L. So sweet.

D. Okay whew.

　　　　(Beat.)

Can I get you a

M. No

D. Are you sure

M. I said no

　　　　(Silence.)

D. Do you want to / dance

M. I'm not feeling so well I'm not feeling / so

D. Oh okay

M. So yeah

> (**L** *nudges her.*)

I mean sure yeah okay
I'd like to
You know
Dance with you

> (*They attempt to dance.*)

> (**L** *takes a picture.*)

L. Omygosh you guys look so cute
You look so freaking cute right now.

D. Will you send it to me?

L. Totes

> (*She hands him her phone.*)

Put in your number

> (*He does.*)

> (**L** *sends it.*)

> (**M** *closes her eyes.*)

> (**D** *looks at his phone.*)

D. Oh yeah look at that

L. So freaking cute

D. Do you mind if I send this to my mom?

M. Your / what

L. Of course not of course she

M. Of course not of course

> (**D** *sends it to his mom.*)

> (**L** *takes a selfie with* **M**, *making sure to get* **D** *in the background.*)

L. This is the night

M. This is the night

D. *(Looking up.)* Like that song

L. What song

D.

    THIS IS THE MOMENT

L. I said "this is the night."

M. "Night."

D. Not "moment"?

L. Yeah "night."

M. Yeah no

D. Oh.

    Well I love that song

    I did that song in the talent show, you know, I got to sing that song

L. Oh wow gosh cool where

D. Here…

    You missed it?

M. Sorry

L. We missed it

M. We missed it

D. oh

L. But we bet you were great

M. Yeah great

L. So great

       (Silence.)

       *(***D*** *sighs contentedly.)*

D. I could die tonight.

M. What?

D. I could die.

L. Why do you

M. Why would you

L. Say

D. *(Bopping unconsciously to the music.)* I'm at Hoopcoming here

    with the smartest and / prettiest

M. oh

D. Girl in the school

>*(He smiles.)*

And her twin who is also the prettiest

L. sure yeah okay

D. Is here with my brother.

Who was too scared to ask anyone to Hoopcoming
'til I told him

You gotta lean into the fear

Lean into it hard

If you lean into it hard enough

Fast enough

"Boldness has genius, power, and magic in it"

L. *(To M.)* Magic

D. Yeah magic

L. So true

D. *(Still bopping.)* That's a quote

I didn't make that up it's a quote

I'm doing this course

My biological dad signed me up for this course

And at first I was mad

He invited me to his "graduation" which was kind of his
"graduation" but also kind of a "recruitment meeting"

And I was kinda uncomfortable

With all these like grown-ups with problems like
drinking or dead children or no job

But I figured "what the hell"

It's summer "what the hell"

Besides it was right after

Anyway

it changed me

It did

It changed me

I didn't use to see positive

I didn't use to see possible

What I did use to see was fat and ugly and fat arms
and fat hands and bad skin and no dad and a brother
with cystic fibrosis and okay at school but probably a
future alone choking to death on a pretzel in my mom's
basement watching reruns of *Cheers*

L. What's *Cheers*

D. It's a show

L. About Cheerleaders?

D. No

Old people like it

My biological dad has like

Tapes and tapes

It's about bars.

And Boston.

And loneliness.

> *(Beat.)*

> *(Back to dancing:)*

But

I learned that that's deadly

That thinking is deadly, you know?

You gotta try

You gotta go after things

You gotta GO

DO

GO

DON'T FEAR PAIN

And it worked

It works

I'm smart

I'm young

I lost thirty pounds

I'm not fat anymore

(maybe my hands)

But not *me*
I'm smart
I'm young
I'm here
With my brother
With the smartest and prettiest girl in my class
This *is* the moment
This is it
I could die happy
tonight
Because I conquered
My
Fear.

> (**M** *and* **L** *are weirdly entranced.*)

And I'm going to college did I tell you I'm going to

> (*They snap out of it.*)

M. Yeah

L. Oh wow yeah
That's so great

M. That's *so* great

D. Did I tell you?
I told you
I talk too much
Sorry
I'm sorry
I talk too much
My mom
Nevermind.

Hi.
Hi.
Do you want to dance again?

M. My feet kinda hurt.

D. It's those shoes I bet

M. Yeah

D. Your feet are so small

M. Not really

D. They are

L. Not really

They're my feet too and they're seven and a half

D. They look so small

So dainty and small

So delicate and small

You have such pretty feet

I read about

In History?

In this handout on China?

(He waits for them to chime in.)

L. Ohhhhh you mean foot binding

M. *(About* **D.***)* Gross

D. Right?

M. *(To* **L,** *still about* **D.***)* Gross gross / gross

D. Right

Right.

We've come a long way.

Globally.

(Beat.)

I'm gonna get a cookie

Do you want a cookie?

M. Sure

L. mmmm

And some punch

D. Okay cool I'll be back with three cookies

L. and punch

D. Three cookies and punch

Back in a jiffo

(He exits.)

L. It's too easy
    Here

       (She hands a tiny plastic baggie to **M.***)*

    When he gets back
    put this in his punch

       *(***M*** stares at the baggie.)*

M. I can't believe I'm about to say this
    Am I about to say this?
    Yes
    I am.
    I am about to say this:

    I can't.

L. What?

M. He's gross but I can't

L. You can

M. I can't

L. What you feel bad?

M. He's *sad*
    He's just *sad*
    I can't.

L. He's got your spot
    He's got your Future
    See that waddling pair of pants?
    That looks like it's waddling towards the snack table?
    It's not.
    It's waddling towards your Future.
    It's waddling away with your Future.

M. He's like *hopeful.*
    That's just

L. Dramatic irony

M. No, *sad.*

L. Same thing.

M. He's kind of like

I can't believe I'm about to say this
He's kind of like

> *(Confused that this word is coming out of her mouth:)*

Inspirational

L. What?

M. Not to me.
But you know, potentially.
To the world at large.

L. He's still fat

M. Not really

L. Uh-huh

M. (maybe his hands)

L. His whole *person*
His *persona* is fat
He takes up *space*
Takes up space that doesn't *belong* to him
Space that belongs to *others*
That is the definition of fatness.

M. I guess

L. Literally that's the definition.
Space-taker.
Look it up.

M. I guess.

L. He's fat in the *soul.*

> *(A squeal from the direction* **D** *went.)*
>
> *(They turn.)*
>
> *(Minor commotion.)*

M. What's that?

L. Maybe he ate the chaperones

M. Stop

L. Or the Table
Or wait wait

> *(She cranes her neck.)*

M. What
　　Can you see

L. I can see it

M. See / what?

L. Yup that was definitely

M. What

L. The sound of him eating Your Future.

　　　　(Beat.)

M. There are *people* here
　　There are all of these

　　　　(Beat.)

　　It's a stupid idea

L. It's *not*
　　We discussed this
　　That's why the brother
　　The Punch then the pocket
　　Brother's coat pocket
　　I stashed it already
　　A second small bag?
　　When I checked our coats
　　It's already there
　　It's perfect
　　It's fine

　　　　(She holds it out again.)

M. You do it then

L. It's not for me it's

M. For me and I say I

L. (selfish)

M. What

L. I said selfish.
　　You and then me
　　That's what it's been
　　Always you and then

M. You
    But I

L. Can

M. No I

L. Can
    It's for you *then* for me
    That's what it's been
    Always you and

M. I know

L. For your *future*

M. I know

L. For *our* future

M. I know

L. And you heard him
    He said he could die
    Tonight
    So we're helping him
    Die happy
    Isn't that what he wants?
    What anyone wants?
    To die
    Happy?

M. But his brother

L. is at fucking death's door
    Did you hear that cough?
    Did you see it?
    On my neck?
    On my fucking neck?
    Vile disgusting gross spit on my neck?

M. No one's going to believe he offed his own brother
    it's stupid
    They're *brothers*

L. Uh duh Cain and Abel

M. it's a stupid idea

L. *it's not / stupid*

>   *(A scream. Musical-ish?)*
>
>   *(**L**, startled, drops the baggie.)*
>
>   *(They watch.)*
>
>   *(**DIRTY GIRL** dances across the stage by herself. Weird, uninhibited. Like no one is watching. She is not wearing semi-formal wear. She is wearing what she always wears. She scream-sings along to whatever song is playing.)*

M. It's a joke
It's a joke
look at her
what made us think that she knows anything special
it's a joke

L. It's not
a joke

>   *(**D** comes back, balancing three cups of punch and holding two cookies carefully wrapped in napkins.)*

D. Here we are punch. And
Two. Cookies.
(In his best French accent.) Ma'moiselles.

>   *(Oh shit the bag's still on the floor.)*
>
>   *(**L** conceals it with her foot.)*
>
>   *(**D** looks at **L**'s awkwardly placed leg.)*
>
>   *(**L** corrects her stance. Now she's standing normally on top of the bag, just at a weird distance from the others.)*

L. Look over there!

>   *(**D** does. She scoops up the bag.)*

What was that noise?

D. Someone saw a rat under the snack table

>   *(**M** and **L** look down at their cookies.)*

    (Beat.)

L. None for you?

D. I'm allergic to tree nuts.

M. To peanuts?

D. To tree nuts. Nuts from trees?

L. Peanuts grow on trees?

D. No peanuts aren't tree nuts
    Peanuts are fine.
    But walnuts, hazelnuts, Brazil nuts
    Almonds, pistachios, cashews
    They'll kill me.

L. Really

M. (Stop)

D. It's true!
    I asked if they had any others
    They got these 'cause more kids are allergic to peanuts
    That's okay
    I used to be afraid of social situations involving snack foods because of my allergy to tree nuts but
    NO FEAR, right?

        (He shows them the lanyard tucked under his shirt.)

    I've got an EpiPen and I know how to use it.

M. Huh

L. It's that bad?

D. I once licked a cashew and it sent me to the hospital for three days. Just licked it, you know? Didn't even put the whole thing in my mouth

L. Wow

D. And my face got all puffy, like –

        (He blows up his cheeks, like a pufferfish.)

    Last week I picked up a walnut with both pinkies just to see what would happen and I didn't die but my hands puffed up. I still can't bend my pinky knuckles.

My counselor says that's why no matter how much weight I lose I'm still fat in my head – I mean why I think I'm fat in my head, because there's some sort of unconscious association going on with food and death and also maybe that's why I use food to address anxiety, because there's this unconscious association with food and death and I've got an unconscious death wish

I'm talking a lot

I talk a lot

My mom (says)

This isn't interesting

For other people

It makes them think I'm fragile

I'm not fragile

Or maybe

I *was* fragile

But now I have NO FEAR

I GO

I DO

I GO

I'm going to stop talking now.

L. You have an unconscious death wish?

D. I mean not now

    It's conscious

    Once you figure out something unconscious

    It's not unconscious anymore

    It's just information

    But sure

    Doesn't everyone?

L. You guys should dance

M. / I don't want

D. Okay

       (**L** *takes their punch cups and pushes them toward the "dance floor."*)

*(Which basically means she pushes them two feet
forward in the space.)*

(Because it's a gym.)

*(**L** exits as **M** and **D** dance.)*

(They are both horrible dancers.)

*(**M** holds but does not eat her cookie.)*

D. You look really pretty

M. uh thanks

    I mean thanks

D. You're a really good dancer

M. I'm not

D. you are

M. I'm good at most things but dancing is not one of them

D. *(Thinks she is flirting.)* Oh yeah?

    Like what are you good at

M. English

    And Math

    And History

    And Music

    I mean Music Theory

    But also Music Performance

    And Physics

    And Chemistry

    (all the sciences really, but I'm real good at Chem)

    And Tennis

    And Crafting

    And delivering meals to the elderly

    And World Peace (model UN)

    And Track

    I run Track.

D. Wow

    I

    Wow

M. So yeah
    But not dancing
    I'm smart
    I'm the smart one
    (she stayed back a year)
    But L is the graceful one
    She does ballet

D. I don't think so

M. That's probably cuz you can't tell us apart
    'Cause we're twins
    And we're Asian
    it's like double hard for white people

D. I can tell you apart

M. Sure

D. I can

M. No you can't
    We switch all the time
    We never get caught

D. Well I can tell

M. *(No.)* Mmm

D. I can

M. You can't because ha I'm not M I'm L

D. What

M. I'm L

D. No you're not

M. We switched hair flowers when you weren't looking

D. Stop it
    You're M

M. You're *sure*

D. I'm sure

M. You're *sure?*

        (**D** *looks at her, considering.*)

    See

*(**D** looks at her again.)*

(Something clicks.)

D. No you're her.

M. *who*

D. M.

You're M

M. How do you know?

D. Because I like you.

*(**M** laughs uncomfortably.)*

M. And you don't like my sister

D. Well not like

M. Like me

D. Like you

Like *like* her

M. Ohmygod we're seventeen you don't have to talk like we're twelve

D. It's my inner fat kid

He's like, stunted.

(From nowhere, he busts out an awesome dance move.)

(She laughs. This surprises both of them.)

M. That was

D. I have no idea where that

M. Cool

It was cool

D. I think that was him

My inner fat kid

Busting a move.

(Beat.)

M. So you like me

D. I do

That's why I can tell

> *(She's kind of impressed.)*
>
> *(He sees this, and smiles.)*

Also I'm not white

> *(Wrong move.)*

M. Oh yeah
You're

D. I've got a tribal ID and everything
Wanna see?

> *(He pulls out the lanyard with his EpiPen, which
> also has some sort of ID card attached.)*

M. You wear it around your neck?

D. I call it my lifeline

M. Your lifeline

D. It's got two things that saved me
Or one that did and one that can
This and *this*
I was out for two weeks at the end of last year?

M. Oh
Uh

D. You don't remember

M. sorry

D. It's okay
No one did
No one would
Which is probably why
I tried to kill myself?
Um
that sounds
No
No
I tried to kill myself
I took a bottle of um
Tylenol

Like a whole bottle and I
sat in the backseat of my mom's Subaru
And I closed my eyes
And I felt myself getting heavier and heavier
But lighter and lighter
And it's gonna sound nuts but I saw
I swear
It's gonna sound nuts but I saw
this um Indian Chief?

M. How did you know he was a Chief?

D. I just knew
In the way that when you're dying you know stuff
Or the way I knew you weren't your sister
I just knew
That this guy was my
Whoa
it was Whoa
You know
And he said

WAKE UP
WAKE UP
I'M YOUR GREAT GREAT GRANDFATHER
AND YOU NEED TO WAKE UP
YOU'RE THE ONLY ONE LEFT
ONLY ONE
ONLY DROP
ONLY GRAIN
ONLY FLECK
ONLY
YOU GET IT
AND IF YOU DIE NOW
LIKE THIS
I'M GONNA COME FIND YOU IN HELL
AND MAKE SURE YOU BURN

SLOWLY
FOREVER
And I was like
Uhhhhh
Isn't Hell for Christians?
And he was like
NOPE
THERE'S A SPECIAL KIND OF HELL
SPECIAL NATIVE AMERICAN HELL
FOR KIDS LIKE YOU
CHICKENS
FOR FAT BABY CHICKENS
WHO GO OUT LIKE CHICKENS
SO
WAKE UP
WAKE UP

And I was like
Can't I just die?
And he was like
IT'S NOT ABOUT YOU
DO YOU THINK I'D BE TALKING TO YOU IF I HAD
OPTIONS
YOU OWE ME
WAKE UP
WAKE UP
WAKE UP
NOW

M. whoa

D. And I did
In a puddle of
(it was gross)
And I asked my mom if we were, if we had any
And she said "nuh-uhn"
And I asked "what about Dad"

And she said "yeah maybe that would explain"
And I asked "explain what"
And she was like "nothing ask him"
And I did and he wrote back
And he gave me a name
And I went on the internet
And found it
I found him: My Great Great Grandpa
Right there on the internet

And then I found *them*
And at first
I was scared?
That I might not
fit in
(you know
'cause the way that I look?)
That they might not
want me
at all
but they were so
they were so
they were all just
so nice.

And there's this like fund?

M. fund?

D. This scholarship fund?
And no one's applied in like years
Because no one's left
It's just me and twelve senior citizens left in our group
in our Nation
Our Tribe
And they said to apply
('Cause my mom
she can't really pay?)

They said
it's okay that I'm new
they're just
happy for me getting in
happy for me being here
happy I'm finally
finally home.
And long story short
Or not short but you know

I'm going.

I'm the first one in my family
Who's going to college
Which makes me like *different*
But for the first time
I feel
Um
Connected?
You know
Even if it's only one half of one half of one half of one
half
And I think that's why when my biological dad invited
me to his "graduation"
And I hadn't left the house in two weeks
And we hadn't talked in two years
I went
because I
finally
felt like I
had Something.

> *(Beat.)*

> *(He exhales.)*

Whew
So I've never told anyone that
Because it sounds you know

M. Crazy?

D. Crazy

M. Like really crazy

D. Like Dirty Girl Crazy

M. Why did you say that?

D. Because that's the bar around here for crazy

>   (**L** *interrupts them.*)

L. Having fun?

>   (**D** *smiles.*)

D. Yeah

M. *(Surprised.)* Yeah

>   (**L** *hands them both punch.*)

>   (**M** *eyes it.*)

L. You guys look hot
   Are you thirsty?

D. Yeah thanks

>   (*Before he can drink,* **M** *drops her cookie in his cup.*)

L. What are you

D. Um

M. Sorry
   Sorry
   That was weird

L. *Why would you do that*

M. My hand was getting tired
   From holding it
   The cookie

L. *So you*

D. It's okay

M. You can't drink it now right?
   It's like poison
   That cup is like poison
   Because of the tree nuts

D. Uh yeah

> *(He looks down at the cup.)*
>
> *(**L** looks daggers at **M**.)*
>
> *(Even **D** notices.)*

Maybe I should check on my brother
See if he's
Yeah

> *(He exits.)*

M. He told me

L. Who cares

M. He told me

L. *Who cares*

M. He wanted to kill himself

L. Great

M. No *actually*

L. Great I said great

M. And this dream
With this
Native American / Chief who

L. Stop.
You are not.
You are not going to do this
Relate to me some stupid story
From some stupid *stupid*
Standing in the way
Of your future
Our future
That I am trying to save
for us

M. But

L. What do you *like* him?

M. That's not what / I'm

L. Then stop

He's nothing
He's nothing
No less than
If nothing is zero
He's like negative a million
The only someone who's something to me
In this room
In this town
In this state
In this place
is you
Am I wrong?

>> *(Beat.)*

M. You're not wrong

L. okay then

M. okay then

L. okay

M. okay

L. Okay

M. Okay.

>> *(**D** enters.)*

D. He's doing okay.
But I should maybe take him home
So he can get in the Vest

L. So soon?

M. Do you have to?

D. I should
Yeah
Family

L. Family is everything

D. It is

L. Yeah it is

>> *(Beat.)*

M. You could come back

D. Mom's working graveyard.
　　I should stay there
　　So he's not home alone
　　In the Vest

L. Or
　　We could go with you

D. *(To* **M.***)* You don't wanna stay?

L. We could all go
　　Together

D. It's kinda boring
　　My house
　　There's not much to do

L. Hoopcoming blows anyway.
　　M and I
　　Were thinking

M. We were (?)

L. There's something fun
　　We could do

D. There is?

　　　　　(**L** *steps close to* **D.** *She thinks she is being seductive,
　　　　　and maybe she is. But it's also kinda confrontational
　　　　　and weird.)*

L. The three of us
　　Yeah
　　While he's doing the Vest
　　The three of us
　　But
　　It would require

　　　　　(She pauses. For drama.)

D. Yeah?

M. Yeah?

　　　　　(**L** *takes a step closer to* **D.** *Their faces are really
　　　　　close. Sexy-weird.)*

L. Total. Privacy.

> (**D** *looks at* **M.** **M** *looks at* **L.**)

M. Okay

L. Okay

M. Okay

D. Uh
  Sure
  I mean
  Snacks!

M. What?

D. We could stop and get snacks
  There's a new cookie place
  Down the block from my house
  I haven't gone in
  On that new part of Elm with the condos?
  It looks like the kind of place that might have
  Gluten-free-nut-free-vegan-type cookies
  Like hypoallergenic cookies
  For the new Rich people and their hypoallergenic dogs
  That's what we call it
  Rich People Cookies
  We could go there
  To Rich People Cookies

M. What's it actually called?

D. Peaches I think
  No, Peaches 'n' Cream

L. No way

M. Really?

D. Yeah why?

L. M's favorite dessert

D. No way
  That's a thing?
  Like an actual thing?

L. It's an actual thing

D. I thought it was just like
a *flavor.*
What is it?

L. Peaches. With Cream.

D. Oh sure that makes sense.
What a coincidence

L. Isn't it though

D. Like magic

L. Like *magic*

(**DIRTY GIRL** *scream-sings again.*)

(*They watch as she dances.*)

9. Basement

*(**D**'s basement. Through a door, the sound of the Vest [loud, rapid vibration] and occasional coughing. A stack of VHS cassettes.)*

*(**D**, **M**, and **L**. On the beat-up sofa are piled four coats and two tiny artisanal-looking shopping bags with "PEACHES 'N' CREAM" in beautiful curlicued script. Brown-crafty tissue paper poking out the top. One bag with a white ribbon tied around the handle.)*

D. *(Calling.)* You okay?

(Silence, except for the sound of the Vest.)

Hey you okay in there?
(To the girls.) He's embarrassed 'cause his voice sounds all shaky when he's in the Vest
(Calling.) You okay?

(No answer.)

Come on, I need to know you're okay.

(Beat.)

Knock twice for yes.

(Beat.)

(Then, slowly, two knocks.)

He's okay.
(Calling.) Knock three times if you need anything, okay? And I'll come help.

(Two knocks.)

(Beat.)

*(**D** turns to the girls.)*

D. Um.

Thanks for hanging out with me. Us.

(He looks at the bags.)

That place, wow

Never seen so many cookies
My mom says when you're rich you have options
I think she meant jobs
But it applies to cookies also

> *(The sound of the Vest amps up a bit – more rapid*
> *vibrations.)*

L. How long will he

D. at least twenty
sometimes when it's bad, half-hour
if it's *real* bad, oxygen, hospital, tubes the whole
but I don't think that's tonight
tonight's prob'ly a half-hour Vest kinda night

M. Why don't you have what he's got?

D. We've got different dads.

L. So he doesn't get a tribal ID?

D. Nope only me.

> *(L sniffs the air – yuck.)*

sorry, the
it's worse when he's nervous
(I said that already)
I think there's a can of air

> *(He looks for some air freshener. Realizes.)*

it's in there with him.

L. Do you have any like *candles*?

D. No! 'cause his oxygen tank?
no open flame
don't want the house to

> *(He makes a "blow up" gesture.)*

M. That wouldn't happen

D. huh?

M. Oxygen burns but it doesn't explode
only old people die in oxygen fires
the old and the slow

D. oh

> (**L** *examines the stack of tapes.*)

L. These are so funny
  They're like little faces

> (*She holds a tape in front of her face, white spools out, so they look like eyes.*)

D. Huh oh yeah

> (*He puts one in front of his face.*)

L. Ohmygod you look like a robot

D. I do?

L. Totes like a robot

> (**D** *does an awkward robot dance.*)

D. (*Robot voice.*) well – what – should – we – do?

> (*He drops the tape and looks at* **M.**)

> (**M** *looks at* **L.**)

> (**L** *looks at* **D.**)

> (*Beat.*)

> (*He looks down at the tape.*)

  Um

  Do you wanna watch *Cheers*?

M. Sure

> (**D** *pops in a VHS cassette.*)

> (*The theme song starts playing.**)

---

*A license to produce *Peerless* does not include a performance license for "Where Everybody Knows Your Name" (the *Cheers* theme song). The publisher and author suggest that the licensee contact ASCAP or BMI to ascertain the music publisher and contact such music publisher to license or acquire permission for performance of the song. If a license or permission is unattainable for "Where Everybody Knows Your Name," the licensee may not use the song in *Peerless* but should create an original composition in a similar style or use a similar song in the public domain. For further information, please see the Music and Third-Party Materials Use Note on page iii.

(They sit and watch.)

(Muffled dialogue and laughter.)

(**D** *laughs.*)

L. I don't get it

D. There was this blonde lady
but now it's a brunette
And that one guy, he's dumb

L. She looks familiar

D. She's a spokeslady for Jenny Craig

L. Who's Jenny Craig

D. It's a weight loss club
my mom belongs

(**L** *raises an eyebrow.*)

L. Your mom

D. Well we go together
It's pretty cool
I wrote about it in my application essay

M. You wrote about a weight loss club?

D. About how it brought us together
About how like *trials* can bring family together

L. *(Is this about the episode or the room?)* This is boring

D. They pretty much only hang out at the bar

(**L** *rolls her eyes.*)

L. Old people are weird

(**M** *stares at the bit of his lanyard sticking out.*)

M. How does it work?

D. What the

M. Yeah

D. Oh sure

(He pulls out the EpiPen.)

As soon as you know you've been
you know

exposed
you grab it like this with your fist

> (*He takes the EpiPen off the lanyard and makes a fist around the pen.*)
>
> (**L** *mimics him.*)

L. Like this?

D. No like

L. Show me
   I wanna
   I wanna try
   Show me

D. You just grab
   With your fist
   Like this

> (**D** *clasps her hand around the EpiPen.*)
>
> (**L** *leans in.* **D** *is nervous.*)

L. Then?

D. That's it really
   Then you just

> (*Without warning, he brings her fist down sharply, violently toward his thigh.*)
>
> (**L** *and* **M** *flinch.*)

L. Holy shit

M. Are you

L. Did you

D. Oh sorry
   didn't mean to scare you
   there's a safety

L. A safety

D. The blue thing

L. That was

M. Terrifying

L. Sexy

D. Huh?

L. Is it sharp

D. What the needle?

L. Yeah

D. very

> *(He mimes stabbing himself in the heart and fake-dying.)*
>
> *(L giggles.)*

L. Does it have to go

> *(She puts her finger on his thigh, where he "stabbed.")*

D. in your thigh
Yeah

> *(He notices that she hasn't moved her finger.)*

Uh
the muscle
it's like crucial
to do it in muscle
uh
sometimes people accidentally
stab their own thumbs
it's disaster

> *(And now her whole hand is there, on his thigh.)*

my uh doctor showed me this picture
um
a boy with no thumb 'cause he accidentally
you know
and it cut off the blood flow
and they had to um amputate?

> *(L gets closer.)*

L. mmmm
Have you ever had to

D. once

L. and

D. I couldn't
    um

L. What

D. I couldn't um do it?
    even tho' I knew I'd die

L. huh

M. What happened?

D. My um
    mom was there
    I couldn't do it
    So she

M. She saved you

D. I was afraid
    but now

L. No Fear.

D. Right
    yeah

> *(Proud.)*

I could totally do it now.

L. That's so hot.

D. *(Looking at* **M.***)* You think so?

L. M?

D. You think?

L. M don't you think?

> *(***M** *says nothing, just looks at him.)*

D. You wanna see?

> *(***M** *takes the EpiPen, looks at it.)*

D. Don't worry you won't kill your thumb
    The safety is

> *(Without warning, she jabs it toward his thigh.
> Swift, violent.)*
>
> *(Beat.)*

(D rubs the spot it landed on [ow] as inconspicuously as possible.)

Um

So yeah

You got it

If I get in trouble I know who to call

(M tosses the pen on the sofa.)

(She picks up a tape and puts it in front of her face.)

M. Can you tell us apart now?

(She tosses one to L.)

(L giggles and puts it in front of her face.)

Can you tell

Can you really

D. Sure

(M takes off her hair flower, L does the same.)

L & M. And now?

L. Of course he can't

D. Sure

L. Don't be dumb no one can

I haven't taken a math test in years

M. *L*

L. I keep a spare red and she keeps a spare yellow

no one can tell

M. *L*

L. (doesn't matter now)

D. I can though I can

(M and L do some sort of swirly-fancy-stepping to change places.)

(Maybe they duck behind furniture.)

(It would be great if we truly had no idea who was who.)

M. Who am I?

L. And me?

D. You're

M. Well

L. Tell me

M. Who?

>   *(Beat.)*

D. You're M
>   You're you

L. Are you sure

D. Yes I'm sure

M. You can tell

D. I can tell

M. Because you like me

D. You know I do

M. And my sister

D. She's pretty
>   She reminds me of you

>   (**L** *drops her tape.*)

L. Uh I'm right here

D. Sorry
>   I mean you're both
>   Um

L. Are you hungry?

D. Huh?

>   (**L** *steps toward him.*)

>   *(Closer.)*

>   *(Closer.)*

L. You know what we
>   really
>   really
>   really
>   want?

(Beat.)

D. yeah?

L. You do?

D. I mean no?

L. to

D. huh?

L. to

    feed

    you.

        (Beat.)

D. Really?

L. Would you like that?

D. uh you

L. want to feed you

    by hand

D. like

L. by touch

    like a baby bird

D. uh

M. Not yet

L. Yes

M. No

L. Now

D. *(To* **M.***)* No I'm game

    It's okay

M. It is?

D. Sure

    I could eat

    You could uh

    Feed me

    If you want to.

M. I could

D. Yeah

   I'd like that

L. You heard him

> (**L** *gets the bag.*)

D. Oh

   Will you make sure it's the one without

L. Sure

> (*She takes a cookie out of the bag without the white ribbon, shows him.*)
>
> (**D** *turns back to* **M.**)
>
> (**L** *switches out the cookie for one from the other bag.*)

   You're safe with us

D. Great

> (**L** *gives* **M** *a piece of cookie.*)

M. Do you trust me?

> (*He looks at her and smiles.*)

D. I do

> (*He opens his mouth.* **M** *moves closer, but still hesitates.*)

L. Do it

D. Yay Rich People Cookies

M. Are you sure?

L. He said do it

M. Are you / *sure*

L. He said

M. (*Still wavering.*) I don't know that / he's

L. He's *sure*

   do it

D. Uh

M. (*To* **L.**) Wait

D. Are you

L. You and / then me

D. Is everything o

M. Me and / then

D. *(Looks at* **L***, then* **M***, a little confused.)* Hey

> *(***M***, startled by* **D***'s dawning awareness of the situation, pops the piece of cookie in his mouth.)*
>
> *(He smiles and chews.)*
>
> *(Then swallows.)*
>
> *(***M** *leans in. They're almost touching.)*

Um.

Hi.

M. Hi.

D. You didn't eat any tree nuts
tonight right?
'Cause that's

> *(***M** *kisses him – it's sweet.)*
>
> *(Then* **L** *kisses him. Less sweet.)*
>
> *(Offstage, the sound of the Vest kicks up another notch.)*
>
> *(***D** *laughs.)*

This is
I can't believe

> *(Beat.)*

Thanks for
Um
Coming over
And

> *(Beat.)*

Huh

L. Yeah?

> *(He scrunches up his face a little.)*

D. Something tastes
Something's not
Are you sure you

M. I'm sure

D. Because sometimes people
They don't even know

> *(He feels his throat.)*

I think I'm
Oh shit
Oh shit
Oh shit
Oh shit
I think I'm

> *(He reaches for the lanyard, but the EpiPen's not on it.)*

Where is
Where is it

> *(**M** picks it up.)*

Oh good whew

> *(**M** looks at him.)*
>
> *(His hands are shaking.)*

Will you
I'm kinda um
Freaking
I can't

> *(**M** looks at **D.**)*

Please

L. Give it to me

> *(**M** looks at **L.**)*

D. Please
M?

> *(***M** *holds out the EpiPen with her right hand – just out of his reach.)*

L. *(To* **M.***)* What are you

> *(***L** *reaches for it.)*

> *(***M** *avoids her, and holds out her left hand in a "stop" gesture.)*

M

> *(***M** *holds out her left hand again.)*

> *(***M** *keeps extending the EpiPen with her right hand to* **D.***)*

> *(***D** *staggers toward her and takes it.)*

> *(He fumbles with the safety.)*

> *(He can't get it off.)*

D. Oh shit

I

Oh shit

Could / you

> *(***M** *looks at him.)*

M. it has to be you

D. I'm

My hands are

Could you

> *(***M** *looks at* **L.***)*

M. No

D. Will you just take the safety

M. I can't

L. She can't

D. I don't under–

M. NO FEAR right

You said it NO FEAR.

> *(They watch him fumble with the safety.)*

> *(He's confused and hurt.)*

(He drops the EpiPen, which rolls under the couch.)

D. Oh shit

Oh shit

It's okay

There's one in the

Will you go to the kitchen and

M. I can't

I'm sorry

(He's going into shock.)

D. Call

9 1

Somebody call

9

(He claws at his throat – he can't speak anymore.)

*(**M** looks at **L**.)*

L. "Hail."

*(**D** looks up at them, confused.)*

(Then understands.)

*(**M** avoids eye contact.)*

(He falls to the ground.)

(He manages to knock over the stack of VHS cassettes, but that's it.)

(Cassettes everywhere.)

Let's go

*(**L** grabs her own coat and **M**'s, then reaches into a third coat's pocket and grabs a tiny bag identical to the one we saw earlier.)*

*(**M** looks down at **D**, who claws at the air.)*

M. I gave you a chance

I tried

I did

(The sound of three distinct knocks.)

(**L** *tosses* **M** *her coat.*)

L. Let's *go*

(*She pushes* **M** *out and follows.*)

(**D** *tries to cry out but it just comes out a wheeze.*)

(**L** *re-enters, grabs* **D***'s phone, and types something into it.*)

(*She bends down and gets up in* **D***'s face. Close. Scary close. It is very quiet, except for the sound of the Vest through the door.*)

(*Knock knock knock.*)

(**L** *stands up and exits.*)

(*The sound of the Vest through the door.*)

10. Prep

(Outside. Cold.)

(The sound of running. Heavy breathing.)

(L and M stop and catch their breath.)

M. What was that

L. What

M. I thought I / heard

L. it's nothing

M. I

(Headlights. The girls freeze. The car passes.)

L. Car it's a car

M. Car

L. Right

   car

M. Shit oh shit oh shit oh shit

(M grabs her throat.)

L. Take a breath

M. I can't –

L. We should work on our story

M. I can't –

L. Hey *hey*

(She puts a hand on M's face.)

   we were there

   we were *there*

   so we'll have to explain

M. we have to go back

L. are you insane?

M. What if he's okay

   if his Brother

   / he

L. he didn't

    not in time

M. Do you hear that

L. Hear what?

(They freeze.)

(Another car passes.)

M. Oh shit shitshitshit
    We should call 9-1-1
    Say it was a mistake

L. He *saw* us he saw

M. We can say we're / sorry

L. Stop

M. He likes / me

L. *It's too late.*
    The only way / out

M. Fuck

L. The only way / on

M. Fuck

L. is through.

(Beat.)

M. How are you calm?

L. I'm going to help you.
    Like you do for me.
    Like we do when it counts.
    Only someone who's some/thing

M. this is diff/erent

L. it's not.
    look at me
    look at me.
    what do you see?

(A breath.)

M. Me

L. And then me.

You
and then

M. You.

L. let's practice
okay
let's do you first
hey
hey

M. okay

L. yeah?

M. okay

(They stand face to face. Close. Breathe.)

L. "Were you aware that the victim had allergies?"

M. He said something at Hoopcoming
Peanuts right?

L. (Nice)

M. That's why when we went to the bakery

L. "Who went?"

M. We all did

L. "We who?"

M. Him, my sister, and me

L. "And his brother?"

M. The car
He wasn't feeling so good

L. "He wasn't?"

M. He's got this condition
forget what it's called
Ohmygod his poor brother

L. "Back to the bakery."

M. That's why
when we ordered –
there were two separate bags

L. "Because of his allergy?"

M. Right
> That's right

L. "Why didn't you stay?"

M. at Hoopcoming?

L. yeah

M. Like I said
> his brother
> Not feeling so good
> Because of his um

L. "Condition."

M. That's right
> He needed to go home and it seemed such a shame
> We were having um such a good time

L. (don't "um" when you say that it sounds insincere)

M. having such a good time

L. "What time did you get to his house?"

M. 8:09

L. 9:08

M. Right 9:08

L. (Nine just say nine)

M. Nine it was nine
> Around nine
> Nine-ish

L. Now me.

M. "What time did you leave?"

L. Nine-twenty or so
> we weren't there long

M. "And what were you doing?"

L. Watching TV shows
> He had like these
> tapes
> of one set in a bar?

M. "A bar? Were you drinking?"

L. Ohmygod never my mother would kill me

M. *(Pointed.)* "Where is your mother?"

L. (oh shit that's no good okay ask me again)

M. "A bar? Were you drinking?"

L. Not that kinda girl.

M. (That's better. Be careful.)

L. (if they want to talk to her?)

M. (out of town – business)

L. "She left you alone?"

M. "Just for the week"

L. "With no way to reach her?"

M. (Call! We can call.)

L. (can she pull it off?)

M. (she'll have to, from there)
    (how much do we tell her?)

L. (*as little as possible*)

M. "Back to the basement"

L. the basement
    right
    right
    "We weren't there long"

M. "Well why did you leave?"

L. Um

M. What

L. He tried to
    Oh god
    Oh god

M. *(Genuinely curious.)* Tried to what

L. Kiss her

M. "Kiss who?"

L. my sister

M. "your sister?"

L. And then after he tried to um force / her to

M. *(Realizing, as **M.**)* Oh my god

L. *(Getting more into it.)* Oh my god

M. You don't mean

L. But he couldn't
He tried but he couldn't
Because I was there

M. You were

L. There to um save her

M. You saved her?

L. *(Really into it now.)* I don't understand how this could happen
I don't understand how this kind of thing could happen
I don't understand how God would allow

M. Laying it on a bit thick don't you think

L. Yeah
Ixnay on the Od-gay
Ohmygod God in Pig Latin is od-gay. Odd gay. Odd GAY. ODD

> (**M** *clears her throat.*)

"I don't understand how this could happen"
(then tears)

M. You can do that?

L. oh totes

M. How did I not know you can do that?

> (**L** *shrugs.*)

L. I've been practicing lots
like in private

> (*She demonstrates.*)

Wanna try?

> (**M** *does. Fails.*)

You'll get it
It's easy

M. So tears

L. tearstearstears

sadsadsad
blahblahblah

(She sniffles.)

and then
the big kicker

M. the what

L. The big sprinter?

M. the

L. Whatever I'm not good at sports

(She sniffles.)

When my sister wouldn't let him
When she wouldn't let him
He called her a

M. *(As herself, genuinely curious.)* What?

L. he called her

M. a what?

He called me a

L. *her*

M. *(As officer.)* "He called her / a"

L. A dirty chi

M. *(As herself.)* Stop it you can't
that's too far
that's too much

L. it's basically true
All that shit about *China?*

M. That's not the same thing as

L. *And feet?*
Oh come / on

M. people will think that the last thing he did
and
people will think that the last thing he said

L. the big kicker
that's it

(She sniffles.)

(This last part is very, very convincing.)

L. Don't tell his mom?
Ohmygod his poor brother
They've suffered enough
I don't want them to think that the last thing he did
was to

M. No

L. And I know he was sorry, I know

M. You know how

L. 'Cause he stopped
when I made him
he stopped
and he texted

M. / He

L. He texted "I'm sorry"
before
Right before / he

*(**L** starts to cry.)*

M. but he didn't

*(**L** holds up her phone. Drops the act.)*

L. He did.

M. No
no no

L. It's good right?
it's good.
okay your turn again
let's do you
Ready?

11. After

> *(The school bell.)*
> *(Three days later.)*
> *(Afternoon.)*
> *(A parking lot.)*
> (**BF**, *waiting.*)
> (**M** *enters.*)

M. Hey.

BF. Hey.

> *(They sit, not saying anything.)*

You doing okay?

M. fine

> *(Beat.)*

BF. S'nuts

> (**M** *looks at him.*)
> *(He realizes the unintentional bad pun.)*

I mean crazy
S'crazy
Shit.

M. Yeah.

> *(Beat.)*

BF. The irony.
Done in by a baked good.

M. He was really allergic.

> *(Beat.)*
> (**BF** *takes out a Snickers and peels it open.*)

BF. *(Deliberately casual.)* Heard that kid got fired
over at the bakery?

M. Good
Good

He should have
Careless
People who work in food service
Should be careful

>> *(Tiny beat.)*

BF. Yeah

>> (**BF** *takes a bite of Snickers. Chews.*)

M. One hazelnut can be the difference between
Life and Death
People who work in food service
Should know that

BF. Do you think he knew?

>> *(He takes a bite.)*

M. The guy who got fired?

BF. Nah
You know *him.*

>> *(He takes another bite.)*

>> *(Chewing.)*

Do you think he knew when he bit into that cookie

>> *(He swallows.)*

I heard that
Last year
He was out for a month
'Cause he tried to
You know
two bottles of Vicodin

M. Tylenol

BF. What

M. It was Tylenol

BF. Oh.
So
What if he knew

When he reached for that cookie
What if he knew and it wasn't an accident

M. It *was* an accident

BF. I mean it was an accident

M. It was

BF. That you left the bag there yeah
But I guess what I'm saying is
I know you feel
bad
I know you feel
bad but
maybe he
maybe he
wanted

M. He didn't

      (Beat.)

BF. Because if he did something?
Tried something?

M. where did you hear

BF. People

M. What people

BF. Just people.
Don't worry about what his brother is saying

M. uhh *what?*

BF. You mean you don't? Shit
there I go my fat mouth

M. What is he saying

BF. psssh
he's upset
he needs someone to blame
I told him to chill
so he got up in my face
and he called me a bitch
a "little dog bitch"

M. that's redundant

BF. uh

yeah

(Beat.)

M. It was an accident.

BF. Right

Right

You're probably right

Who in their right mind would choose to

like that

(Somewhere, the sound of nibbling.)

*(**M** turns. **BF** doesn't notice.)*

You know

I was pissed

I was kinda um pissed

When I heard you were

Hoopcoming?

But it's hard to be pissed at a dead guy

M. Yeah

(Beat.)

BF. Think you'll get his spot?

M. What?

BF. Do you think you'll

M. I heard you

it's just that that's not on my radar right now?

BF. Not even a little?

M. It's been like *three days*

BF. Heard that this guy in 2001

he died of like cancer.

They took someone else

M. it was his mom

who got cancer

BF. You / sure?

M. He didn't die he deferred

BF. The point is that year They took someone else.

    (The sound of nibbling gets louder. **M** *turns.)*

M. Do you hear that?

BF. Hear what?

M. *that*

BF. There are kids over there, behind that car

M. Eating?

BF. I was gonna say smoking?

M. tiny teeth
    tiny hands
    tiny
    teeth and hands eating

    (She listens.)

    *(***BF*** watches her.)*

BF. You sure you're / alright

M. I'm fine

BF. You're sure

M. I said yeah

BF. WAKE UP

M. Don't yell at me

BF. Huh?

M. Don't yell

BF. Uh I didn't

M. you did

BF. No I WAKE UP

M. Ohmygod *stop*

BF. I don't know what / you're

M. Stop fucking / with me

BF. I'm / not

M. STOP

BF. jeez okay sorry

(Beat.)

M. Sorry, the
　　All the
　　You know
　　Sorry

BF. Yeah sure
　　Right
　　I should get / back to

　　　　(A black feather falls from the sky.)

　　　　*(**M** watches it fall.)*

　　　　(She bends down to pick it up.)

　　　　*(**BF** moves his mouth, but what comes out is the sound of eating. Tiny teeth, tiny hands, tiny teeth and hands eating.)*

　　　　*(**M** stares at him.)*

M. What did you say?

BF. Uh I said you might wanna leave that alone
　　Birds carry all kinds of diseases 'n shit

　　　　*(**M** leaves the feather untouched.)*

M. I have to go now

BF. Are you sure you're

　　　　(She goes.)

12. Mail

(The caw of a large scavenger bird overhead.)

(A thick 10x13 envelope falls from the sky…in front of **BF***. Thud.)*

(Elsewhere, in darkness, a figure in a hoodie spray paints something on the girls' lockers. Then runs.)

13. Early Decision (Round 2)

(Morning.)

(L, by their lockers with the word "LIARS" freshly spray painted across.)

(M enters.)

(Beat.)

(She wipes her finger across the wet paint ["what the fuck?"].)

L. Did you hear?

M. I can't.

L. You heard

M. *I can't*

L. Did you / *know?*

M. *believe*

L. did you know he *applied?*

M. of course not

L. of course
But how did They find / out so fast

M. They're The College
They *know.*

L. And he never let on?

M. "*Historically* Black *College*"
That's what he said

L. That's what he told you

M. That's what he *said*

L. "Historically *Black*"

M. *(Imitating* **BF**.*)* "I don't have the stats for *The College*" he said

L. when

M. in September
"I don't have your softs or your grades or your rank"

L. But he *did.*

M. But he *said*!

L. And what did you say

M. "Don't waste your one shot"

L. (That's good that was good)
   And he seemed to buy it?

M. uh yeah *at the time.*

       (Tiny beat.)

L. *(Does she mean it?)* You couldn't have known

M. *(Upset, replaying.)* "Don't waste your one shot
   Your one early shot
   It's *binding*"

L. It is

M. "Early decision is *binding*"

L. You only get one

M. "You should be strategic"

L. He was.

M. Ohmygod

L. He totally was.

M. *(Dawning realization.)* He played me

L. He did

M. He lied to / me

L. He did

M. He wanted The College

L. He did

M. The whole time

L. the whole fall
   He played you
   you thought he was

M. Safe

L. neutralized

M. *Safe*

L. but
   the whole time

M. He played me

L. He *did*

      (Tiny beat.)

M. But Dirty Girl *said*
    You said that she knew / things

L. *yeah I know*

M. She said I'd get in
    Me and my

      (Beat.)

L. what

M. and my "little dog too"

L. you don't have a dog

M. I thought she meant you

L. *hey*

M. *I* didn't say it
    I thought she meant you
    ohmygod she meant *him*
    "little dog bitch"
    that's what he called him

L. I don't understand
    that's what who called who?

M. The Brother
    That's what the Brother called
    ohmygod
    That's what he called the Boyfriend
    "little dog bitch"

L. that's redundant

M. *I know.*
    She totally knew
    You were right
    holy fuck
    How did she

L. *No.*

(Tiny beat.)

M. No?

(Beat.)

L. she was right about him
so she's right about us
who cares about *how* / she

M. But she didn't say *us*
She only said *me*
Me and my "little

L. She didn't say *not me*

M. But how did she / *know*

L. No.
The real question's not "*how* did she / know"

M. what then

L. no, not "what then?" either

M. no?

L. it's / not

M. not "what then"…

L. no

M. You / mean

L. I mean

M. Not what then

L. not "what *then*"

M. What.

L. *Now.*

(Beat.)

M. How

L. How

M. How

L. How.

(Pause.)

These things happen in clusters

M. What things

L. You know *these*

Teens hurting themselves

The pressure

The guilt

M. No one will believe

I mean two in a row?

L. *Clusters* I swear.

everyone *knows* what happened on Hoopcoming

M. not everyone

L. *Everyone.*

suicide cookie

guilt suicide cookie

that's what they all think

M. *(Looking at the graffitied lockers.)* (Except for the Brother)

L. and everyone *knows* who got in after

everyone *sees* who got the One Spot

M. "the little dog bitch"

L. the pressure

the *guilt*

he'd have to feel guilty

to benefit right?

maybe guilty enough to

> *(L pulls out a baggie of white powder. She holds it up.)*

M. Are you crazy? Put that a/way

L. *(Extending it toward M.)* here

M. before someone

L. take it

M. no

L. I can wait

M. *L*

L. But just so you know someone's coming this way.

(**M** *snatches the bag and conceals it. She's not happy about it, but manages to slap on a bright smile [as does* **L**] *as someone walks by.*)

(*They watch, then drop their smiles.*)

(*Beat.*)

(**M** *hurls the bag at* **L**. **L** *conceals it.*)

(*Beat.*)

L. Stop being so selfish

M. / *what?*

L. You and then me
     that's what it's always been
     you and

M. *I know*

L. he's your boyfriend

M. *ex*

L. well he trusts / you

M. uhhh are you sure?

L. well
     more than me

M. Everything's different
     this week has been weird
     the last time I saw him

L. Ohmygod
     deja vu
     and it's sucking
     it's sucking
     it's sucking
     it sucks
     Do you *like him?*

M. *no*
     it was only pretend
     for safety
     for us

L. I hear the words
   coming out of your mouth / but

M. I'm just saying

L. You're always just saying
   You're saying and saying and saying and

M. *so?*

L. so I'm always the doer
   I'm *doing*
   I *do*

M. he wouldn't, like *that*
   he'd do it by car
   or by gun
   / or

L. How do you know?

M. it's a stupid idea

L. it's not
   I'm not stupid

M. come on, eating poison?
   is that how *you'd* kill your/self?

L. we're not talking me

M. it's not how he'd do it
   not to himself
   that's how someone *else* would do it *to* him

L. ohmygod
   I've got it
   I've got it
   it's good.
   it's *good.*
   it's so freaking good

M. Will you get to the

   (Lights shift as:)

   *(**L** suddenly covers **M**'s mouth with her hand.)*

   *(**L** speaks into **M**'s ear, but though her mouth is moving, all we hear is a different, distorted voice echoing "WAKE UP" through the halls.)*

> (**M** *struggles but can't get away –* **L** *holds her firm.*)
> (**M** *finally* THROWS **L** *off, then:*)
> (*Light shift.*)
> (**L** *looks at her. Normal.*)

L. Are you okay?

M. Fine. I'm fine.
  I mean

> (**M** *collects herself.*)

  What did you say?

> (**L** *looks at her strangely.*)

L. I said
  "everyone knows that D did himself in
  Except the one person who doesn't believe."

> (**L** *looks at "Liars" painted across their lockers.* **M** *follows her eye.*)

M. (*Back on track.*) the Brother

L. is angry
  blames *us*
  but not *just* us
  who else?
  who benefits more?
  who did he fight with, right here in the halls?
  who's getting the spot the *one spot* at The College?

> (*Somewhere, the sound of eating. Faint.*)

M. It's good.

L. It's *good.*

> (*She takes out a second baggie of powder, and holds up both baggies.*)

L. you do the Boyfriend
  and I do the pocket
  the *Brother's* coat pocket
  (or locker whatev)

M. (nuh-unh the locker
   you'd have to break in
   you'd never get near)

L. (so ixnay the locker
   and ixnay the coat)

   They have a backyard
   You do the Boyfriend
   I do the Backyard

M. The Brother's backyard?

L. I go there at night
   and plant the stuff there
   make one little call

M. a tip off

L. a clue

M. to search

L. to find

M. the answer

L. to all of our problems at once

M. tied up in a

L. tight little

M. neat little

L. See?

> *(She holds out the bag.)*
>
> *(This time, **M** takes it.)*
>
> *(The sound of eating goes silent.)*

Things have a way of working themselves out.

14. Crack

(The sound of heavy breathing.)

(M and L, asleep.)

(M tosses.)

(She turns.)

(She tosses.)

(She turns.)

(Maybe, from a distance, we hear the theme song from Cheers.*)*

Crack.

(M shoots up in bed.)

(Looks around.)

(Nothing.)

(She settles back down.)

Crack.

*(D appears. In this dim lighting, we see the outlines of what appears to be a strange, black-feathered costume. Is it a headdress/regalia? Not quite. But suggestive enough of one that it could read as appropriative to those looking, especially in the shadows.**)*

---

*A license to produce *Peerless* does not include a performance license for "Where Everybody Knows Your Name" (the *Cheers* theme song). The publisher and author suggest that the licensee contact ASCAP or BMI to ascertain the music publisher and contact such music publisher to license or acquire permission for performance of the song. If a license or permission is unattainable for "Where Everybody Knows Your Name," the licensee may not use the song in *Peerless* but should create an original composition in a similar style or use a similar song in the public domain. For further information, please see the Music and Third-Party Materials Use Note on page iii.

**Depending on the light, and the angle, what D is wearing reveals itself to be something entirely different and far more solid. At moments it may disappear altogether and all we see is a sad young man. As the reality reveals itself to M, she flickers between fearful defensiveness, intrigue, heartbreak, and terror.

(**M** *wakes up, sees him.*)

(*He turns toward her.*)

M. hey

(*He takes a step toward her.*)

hey.

(*Another step.*)

what are you wearing?

(*Another step.*)

It's *offensive*

(*Another.*)

Crack.

(**D** *pauses, scrunching up his face.*)

(*He touches his throat.*)

(*Then takes another step.*)

Crack.

(*He gags.*)

(*Another step.*)

Crack.

(*He gags again, but keeps moving.*)

(*He is overcome by gagging.*)

(*He doubles over, without air. With one final, silent spasm he heaves up a withered black walnut.*)

(*He looks at it, curious.*)

Is that – is that a walnut?

Crack.

(*He looks up at **M**, then holds it out toward her, an offering.*)

I don't want it.

(*He steps toward her again.*)

M. Stop

> *(He doesn't.)*

  stop or I'll

> *(She tries to wake* **L**, *who doesn't stir.)*
>
> *(He steps closer, almost upon her.)*
>
> *(He leans forward.)*
>
> *(And smiles.)*

D. How.

> *(Darkness.)*

  Crack.

> *(The music stops.)*
>
> *(The thick flutter of wings, then silence.)*
>
> *(Someone fumbles in bed.)*
>
> *(Click.)*
>
> *(**M** turns on the light.)*
>
> *(**D** is gone.* **L** *stands by the window.)*

M. L?

L. M?

M. did you / see

L. did you hear?
  I thought I heard something / outside

M. heard what

> *(**L** shrugs, gets back into bed.)*

L. I was wrong
  wasn't anything there

> *(**M** sees a black feather on the floor. Picks it up.)*

M. he was here

L. who

M. *him.*
  L, I saw him

I *saw*
he was / *here*

L. Shhhh
you were dreaming

M. I / wasn't

L. you were.
just some silly feather from some dirty

M. no

L. prob'ly blew in from outside

> *(**L** takes the feather from **M**'s fingers.)*

M. give it / back

L. M

M. *give it to me NOW*

> *(Beat.)*

> *(**L** extends the feather.)*

> *(**M** takes it.)*

we never should have

> *(Beat.)*

The window is closed.

> *(**L** looks – it's true. And that's weird. But.)*

L. Come back to bed.
Tomorrow's a big day.

> *(**M** looks back at the feather.)*

L. look at me
look at me.

> *(**M** does.)*

what do you see?

> *(A breath.)*

M. me.

L. and then me.
You
and then

M. you.

> (**L** *gently takes the feather away.* **M** *lets her.*)

L. *(Leading her.)* Come back to bed.

M. *(Hesitating.)* tomorrow

L. yes

M. I don't

L. Shhhh

M. I'm not sure
    if we fail

L. we won't

M. but
    if either suspects

L. they don't
    they won't

M. or
    if somebody sees

L. *(Trying to put* **M** *to bed.)* Shhhh
    for our Future
    for *us.*

M. we don't know
    it's not / *safe*

L. *M, we're so close*
    for you
    then for / me

M. *no*

L. *(Pushing* **M** *down.)* if we get through / tomorrow

M. *(Resisting.)* I don't / want

L. let's talk tomorrow

M. that's what I mean
    / tomorrow

L. tomorrow's tomorr/ow

M. no
    I want to talk *now*

L. *(Covering* **M***'s mouth.)* go to sleep

M. *(Pushing off* **L***'s hand.)* no I

> (**L** *slaps her, hard.)*
>
> *(This shocks both of them.)*
>
> *(Beat.)*
>
> (**M** *touches her own cheek.)*
>
> *(She looks at* **L.***)*
>
> *(Something shifts.)*

L. I

I'm sorry I

> *(Beat.)*

M. I want to talk to her.

L. Who

M. Dirty.

L. okay

M. And if after that I don't want

L. Call me after you talk.

> (**L** *puts her hand on* **M***'s.* **M** *looks down at their hands. With fiercest, truest love:)*

Only someone who's something to me

In this town

In this state

In this country

this place

is you

> *(Pause.)*

M. is you

L. is you

M. is you.

L. okay?

M. okay

L. okay.

M. okay.

L. I'm sorry.

M, I'm

(The sound of tiny teeth and hands nibbling.)

(A shadow passes over the window.)

*(**L** turns toward the sound. **M** turns toward the window.)*

M. *(Moving toward the window.)* did you see

L. did you hear

(Beat.)

M. There's somebody out there.

*(**L** joins her at the window.)*

(Someone in a hoodie stands in the darkness. We cannot see his face.)

*(**M** and **L** stand there, watching and watched.)*

15. Consultation

> *(The school bell.)*

> *(**DIRTY GIRL** sits on the floor eating her lunch. Some sort of gray sandwich in a baggie.)*

> *(**M** stands above her, holding a brown paper sack.)*

M. Hey.

> *(**DIRTY GIRL** eats her sandwich.)*

Hey.

> *(**DIRTY GIRL** eats her sandwich.)*

I know you can talk you did it before.

> *(Beat.)*

Caroline.

DIRTY GIRL. *what.*

M. You were right.

point-five deduction.

peaches 'n' cream.

me and my little

> *(**DIRTY GIRL** stares at her.)*

> *(Then pulls out a cigarette.)*

> *(Waits.)*

(Realizing.) I don't have a match.

> *(**DIRTY GIRL** produces a lighter from behind **M**'s ear. Like magic.)*

> *(She tosses it to **M**.)*

Are you allowed to

> *(**DIRTY GIRL** looks at her.)*

> *(**M** lights the cigarette.)*

> *(**DIRTY GIRL** inhales. And exhales in **M**'s face.)*

DIRTY GIRL. Watch out for the Brother

M. The Brother?

DIRTY GIRL. Beware.
   He's watching
   and waiting

M. *(Realizing.)* last night
   he was there
   outside the window
   What will he do?

DIRTY GIRL. *Knock knock.*

        (Beat.)

        (Pointed:)

   Knock.
   Knock.

M. *(Unsure.)* Who's there?

        (A loud KNOCK KNOCK rattles the halls.)

        *(A **GHOSTLY FIGURE** appears.)*

        *(A terrible whisper echoes through the halls as the
        figure walks slowly toward **M**.)*

VOICE. only one left
   only drop
   only grain
   only fleck

        *(**M** backs away.)*

M. It wasn't my fault

        *(**DIRTY GIRL** tsk-tsks.)*

DIRTY GIRL. but you knew

        *(The **GHOST** keeps approaching.)*

   and just when they
   finally
   finally
   found him

VOICE. *one*

M. I didn't mean / to –

VOICE. *only / one*

M. I didn't

DIRTY GIRL. then who?

M. *(To* **GHOST**.*)* I never wanted

DIRTY GIRL. you didn't

M. I

VOICE. *one*

DIRTY GIRL. became
None
became

M. *nonono*
NO

> *(The* **GHOST** *disappears. [Does she push him back into the locker?]* **DIRTY GIRL** *extends her arm in a Nazi salute.)*

DIRTY GIRL. Hail.

> *(***M** *swats her arm down.* **DIRTY GIRL** *laughs, then drapes the arm around* **M**.*)*

What is it you *want?*

M. I
I want to succeed.

DIRTY GIRL. that's nothing
that's all?

M. no I
I want / more

DIRTY GIRL. *more*

M. to be safe
to be free
I want

DIRTY GIRL. yes

M. I want

DIRTY GIRL. *yes*

M. I want
what I *deserve*

DIRTY GIRL. which is?

M. Everything.

DIRTY GIRL. ahhhhh.

M. what?

DIRTY GIRL. I said "ahhhhh."
   and what about *her*?

M. she wants what I

DIRTY GIRL. oh?

M. only someone who's something
   is me
   on/ly me

DIRTY GIRL. *(Brushing* **M***'s cheek.)* are you sure?

       *(***M*** touches her cheek, remembering.)*

   one
   They take one

M. yeah I know
   me and then

DIRTY GIRL. *no no no / no*

M. no?

DIRTY GIRL. *one*
   can't be *both*

M. you mean

DIRTY GIRL. *one*
   can't be *two*

M. but

DIRTY GIRL. She's watching
   and waiting
   What will she do?

       (Beat.)

M. She's watching

DIRTY GIRL. And waiting

M. And

DIRTY GIRL. *She will be you.*

M. She –

DIRTY GIRL. She'll do well
at The College

M. you said *I'd* / get

DIRTY GIRL. which one are you?

M. *I'm the smart one*

DIRTY GIRL. and yet
you still do what *she* wants
it's her and then you

M. me and then *her*

DIRTY GIRL. that's what she says
but then what will she *do?*

>   (*The sound of squeaking from* **DIRTY GIRL***'s
>   pocket.*)
>
>   (*She breaks off a piece of sandwich and feeds her
>   pocket, making gentle clucking sounds.*)

M. How do / I

DIRTY GIRL. *you go*
you do
you go
no fear

M. Will I get what I want?

DIRTY GIRL. We all do in the end

M. *Are you sure?*

>   (**DIRTY GIRL** *looks up.*)

DIRTY GIRL. Don't make me fucking repeat myself.

>   (**M** *extends* **DIRTY GIRL***'s lighter.*)
>
>   (**DIRTY GIRL** *shrugs it off [*"keep it"*].*)
>
>   (**M** *pockets the lighter.*)
>
>   (*Beat.*)
>
>   (**M** *drops the brown paper bag at* **DIRTY GIRL***'s feet.*)

M. It's a fifty
     And an apple
     You know, for your time.

16. Track (2)

(The sound of heavy breathing.)

(Track practice.)

*(**M** running with iPhone.)*

(The sound of nibbling.)

(She stops. It stops.)

(She starts running again.)

(The sound of nibbling, louder.)

(She stops. It stops.)

(She starts running again.)

(The sound of nibbling again. It's really fucking loud.)

(The phone rings. She stops.)

(It rings again.)

(She looks at it.)

(Makes a decision.)

(Picks up.)

*(**L** appears, somewhere else, on the other end of the call.)*

M. Don't do it. It's off.

*(**M** hangs up, disappears.)*

*(**L** stares at her phone in disbelief.)*

*(The sound of nibbling, growing louder and louder as **L** inhales, making a decision.)*

(Turns and goes.)

17. Switch

(The parking lot.)

(Dusk, but overcast. Silhouettes and colors.)

*(***BF*** enters.)*

(We hear [but do not see] a girl speak.)

L/M. *(Offstage.)* Hey

BF. *(Confused.)* hey

L/M. *(Offstage.)* It's me.

*(A Snickers appears in **BF**'s hand. Like magic.)*

(He peels it, takes a bite.)

(A caw from above.)

18. Later

(It's dark.)

(A girl stands outside with a lighter.)

(She lights the lighter.)

(Puts it out.)

(She lights it.)

(Puts it out.)

(She reaches into her pocket and takes out a single black feather.)

(She lights it, and watches it burn.)

19. Morning

>*(The school bell.)*
>
>*(Whispers. Or is it nibbling? It's hard to tell at this point.)*
>
>*(Whatever it is, it's* loud.*)*
>
>**(L** *enters.)*
>
>*(She is wearing her yellow backpack, but her clothes and hair are a mess.)*
>
>**(L** *turns to an unseen student:)*

L. What.

>*(The whispering/nibbling stops.)*
>
>**(M** *enters.)*
>
>*(She is wearing her red backpack. Her clothes and hair look normal.)*
>
>*(They stand, apart from the unseen others.)*
>
>**(L** *looks worried.)*

Did you hear?

M. I can't

L. you heard

M. I *can't.*

L & M. *Where the hell have you been?*

M. I've been calling and call/ing

L. *I've* been calling and call/ing

M. But you never picked up.

L. *(Holding up her phone.)* But my phone never rang!

M. *(Grabbing* **L** *'s phone, suspicious.)* What? Let me see.

>*(**M** checks the phone, clearly upset.)*

L. I was out all night looking / for you

M. I said it was off
　　fuck, L
　　I *said*

*(**M** gets frustrated with the phone, pushes it back at **L**.)*

L. / I know

M. I know that you'll *say*
   you did this for me but

L. *(Confused.)* the / Brother?

M. the *Brother*, the *Boyfriend*
   I said it was *off*

L. but

M. you met him
   the Boyfriend

L. I did/n't

M. you / did

L. Did something / happen

M. *stop.*
   people saw you
   they *saw.*

   you and the Boyfriend
   outside
   after school
   you gave him a Snickers
   he ended up *dead.*
   but how did you get him to
   ohmygod
   did you say you were me?

L. no / I

M. ohmygod
   ohmygod
   ohmygod
   ohmygod
   you said you were me

L. I / didn't

M. WAKE UP

L. I

M. WAKE UP

L. STOP YELL/ING

M. no one's

L. STOP I SAID STOP

>*(The sound of nibbling – but from where?)*

>*(**L** turns toward the sound.)*

>*(**M** watches her.)*

only someone who's something
is you
on/ly you

M. *yeah I know.*

that's what you *say*
but that's not what you *do.*

killing the Brother?
his house up in flames?
the Boyfriend
the Brother
and Hoopcoming too
you *say* it's for me
but it's / really

L. *(Confused.)* but he's alive

M. *(Quick.)* what

L. The Brother
I heard he /got out

M. *the retard's alive?*

L. unconscious
on oxygen
/ hospital

M. *the retard got out?*

L. he's *not / retarded he's got*

M. think he'll wake up?

L. cystic fiber– / *shit*

M. *(In her face, scary.) do you think he'll wake up?*

(**L** *looks at her.*)

L. *(Realizing.) it was you.*

      (**M** *brushes past her.*)

M. *it was you.*

   yellow backpack
   they saw.

L. why would you
   fire?
   that wasn't the plan

M. the plan wasn't good.

L. it / was

M. wasn't

L. it / was

M. Dirty knows things
   She knows.
   one
   they take *one*

L. we know that
   we / know

M. *No.*

      (*Beat.*)

L. no?
   what do you
   what did / she say?

M. *(Ignoring.)* you say you're the doer
   but really you
   push
   you're the pusher

L. for / you

M. you
   all / for

L. *(Horror.) what else did you do?*

      (*Beat.*)

M. *one* can't be both
can't be

L. one?

M. can't be *two.*

L. only someone who's something
is

M. me
only
/ me

L. *LOOK AT ME.*

M. L meant well
she did
did it all for her sister.
"I'm sorry" she texted
"I did it for you."

L. she didn't

M. *she did.*

> (**L** *remembers her phone. She takes it out, looks.*)
> (*And understands.*)

L. no
no / no

M. she left a note to confess
only minutes ago
the Snickers
the fire
the *fake text* from **D**
"check his phone for my prints –"

> (**L** *flings her phone on the floor.*)

L. no no no
no no *no*

> (**M** *starts to cry.*)

M. "it was me
only me.

but I did it for her."

L. it was

   / you

M. *you.*

   but you did it for me.

L. I / didn't

M. did

L. I / didn't

M. did

L. it was / *you*

M. you

L. *you you*

        *(**M** smothers **L**'s mouth.)*

   (Muffled.) / yyy

M. you

        *(**L** throws **M** off.)*

        (They fight. It's ugly – hair, teeth.)

M. *(As they fight.)* Dirty said that I'd get what I

        *(**M** cries out as **L** kicks her off and bites her leg. She draws blood.)*

        (As they fight:)

M. you

L. you

M. you

L. *bitch.*

        *(**M** punches **L** in the back.)*

        *(**L** fakes her out and gets the upper hand again.)*

        *(**L** gets her hands around **M**'s throat.)*

M. I'll get everything

   all of it

   that's what she

        *(**L** squeezes.)*

(And squeezes.)

(And.)

*(Abruptly lets go. **L** falls back in horror.)*

(They crouch, face to face, panting.)

M. *(Heaving.)* They'll know by now.
The College
They'll know.

*(**L**'s phone – still on the floor – rings.)*

I almost forgot
You left your number
when you confessed

*(**M** straightens her clothes.)*

Mail's due any minute.
I'm going home.

*(**M** exits.)*

*(**L** looks at the phone and panics. Sets it on the ground. Takes a few steps away. Hurries back and crushes it with her shoe.)*

(She pulls a red backpack out of her yellow one, tucks the yellow inside.)

20. V

(The sound of heavy breathing.)

*(**M** sits at home, waiting for the mail. She does not hear the sound.)*

(She flicks on Dirty Girl's lighter.)

(Puts it out.)

(Flicks it on.)

(Puts it out.)

(Flicks it on −)

(Outside, the caw of a large scavenger bird.)

(Thud.)

*(**M** leaps to her feet and opens the door.)*

(She sees the stuffed-to-the-brim 10x13 envelope.)

(She grabs it and slams the door.)

(She tears open the envelope and reads:)

M. "We are pleased to inform you that…"

YES.

YES.

I GO

I DO

I GO

I

(She squeals/screams and does a little dance. Maybe [unconsciously] this reminds us of Dirty Girl.)

(As she does the above, the door swings open, unnoticed.)

*(The **BROTHER** stands in the doorway.)*

(He looks a lot like D − but sicker, with no glasses.)

*(He looks a lot like **D** because he's played by the same actor.)*

(He looks sicker because he's dying, and dragging a three-foot-tall oxygen tank on wheels.)

(A two-pronged nasal cannula is taped to his face, and long coils of tubes run up to the tank.)

(It's an effort for him to breathe – heavy, difficult breaths in…out…in…out.)

(He shuts the door – click.)

(She turns and sees him.)

M. *What.*

*(The **BROTHER** enters, breathing his painful, funny-awful breaths.)*

(In…out…in…out.)

What is it you want?

(He moves toward her.)

(It takes everything he has to drag his oxygen tank behind him.)

(He coughs.)

(Sniffing.) You smell like shit.

(He slowly drags himself in a few more feet.)

(The cough turns into a coughing fit. He finally spits out a tiny amount of mucus.)

(He bends over, lightheaded.)

Gross

That's just gross.

(He begins to turn the valve on the tank: hissssssssssssssss.)

(Cough, cough.)

Are you trying to start a fire?

(Hands shaking, he takes out a match.)

(She laughs.)

Oxygen *doesn't explode.*
does nobody else pay attention in Chem?

> *(He coughs – the match goes flying.)*
> *(He falls to the ground, reaching for the match, but right before he does – M steps on it.)*

that's so sad.

> *(She bends down and gets in his face.)*

Oxygen won't do shit.

> *(She kicks the matchbox away.)*

singe the carpet a bit
maybe trap *you*
only old people die in oxygen fires
the old and the sick and the weak and the slow
but I can walk out
walk right out with *this*

> *(She waves the packet.)*

Don't believe me?

> *(He looks up.)*

Here.

> *(She tosses him **DIRTY GIRL**'s lighter.)*

I'm real good at Chemistry.

> *(Hissssssssssssssssssssssssssssssssssssssssssssssssssssssssssss sssssssssssss.)*
> *(He looks at her, and coughs.)*

BROTHER. I think you're right.
M. I know I am.

> *(He coughs again, and again.)*
> *(Then raps on the tank: knock knock.)*
> *(And smiles.)*

BROTHER. Good thing it's not oxygen.

(He pulls up the end of the nasal tubing, which is not [and never was] connected to the tank of L.P.G. [Liquid Propane Gas].)

M. But

(He flicks the lighter.)

(BLINDING LIGHT.)

(Silence.)

(Then, the sound of thousands of tiny teeth and hands. It gets louder, then fades, as charred bits of paper float down from the sky.)

21. The Future

(Outside.)

(Trees and brick.)

(Colonial columns.)

(Everything looks bright and expensive.)

(L stands on the Quad in a red backpack.)

(In awe.)

(She breathes in the clean air, rich with history.)

(A **PREPPY GIRL** *enters – she looks exactly how* **DIRTY GIRL** *would look if she cleaned up.)*

PREPPY GIRL. Excuse me!

L. Yes?

PREPPY GIRL. Do you know how to get to Webster?

L. I'm a Freshman too, sorry.

PREPPY GIRL. No worries.

*(***PREPPY GIRL** *starts to go, but turns back.)*

You look familiar, have we met?

L. I don't think so

PREPPY GIRL. Maybe at Orientation?

Did you do Outward Bound?

L. No.

PREPPY GIRL. I did Outward Bound.

L. Oh.

PREPPY GIRL. yeah…so

L. I probably remind you of someone from home.

PREPPY GIRL. Must be it

(She extends her hand.)

I'm Debbie.

*(***L** *takes* **PREPPY GIRL***'s hand.)*

L. M

PREPPY GIRL. Like Emma?

L. Just "M"

PREPPY GIRL. Like the letter

That's cool

L. Where are you from?

PREPPY GIRL. Cali

You?

L. Midwest.

I've never been to California

PREPPY GIRL. Oh it's the *best*

You *have* to go.

L. I want to

yeah

I think I want to

PREPPY GIRL. Then you will.

L. You think?

PREPPY GIRL. Absolutely.

you know what they say, "where there's a will"

> (*Beat.*)

What's your major?

L. I was thinking Pre-med but I'm not sure.

PREPPY GIRL. I'm Pre-med!

We could have like allllllll our classes together.

> (*The school bell rings. But instead of the bright alarms of high school, it's the deep, resonant ring of bells in a chapel tower. It's that kind of College.*)

I should try to find Webster. I'm meeting my brother for lunch.

L. Your brother goes here?

PREPPY GIRL. Yup. Sibling preference.

> (*She leans in, a "secret."*)

I'd never've gotten in if not for him.

L. Me too.

PREPPY GIRL. Your brother's here too?!

L. Sister.

And no, she died.

PREPPY GIRL. Oh

L. There was an accident

PREPPY GIRL. Sorry I

L. It's okay.

I just meant –

I wouldn't be here without her

I owe all this to her.

PREPPY GIRL. I'm sure she'd be proud of you

L. Yeah I think so.

Anyway I'm trying not to look back

I'm trying to not get too stuck in the past

'Cause we're here

We're *here.*

PREPPY GIRL. Yeah!

And we're like, the *Future,* you know?

L. The Future.

PREPPY GIRL. That's us!

　　　(Beat.)

If you do Pre-med get ready, my brother says first year
is *brutal*

L. He's Pre-med too?

PREPPY GIRL. applying to med school now. I thought
getting in *here* was tough.

　　　(**PREPPY GIRL** *sees someone across the Quad and
　　　waves.*)

Kripa! Kripaaaaaaaa!

Do you know where Webster is?!

　　　(**PREPPY GIRL** *turns back to* **L.***)*

Nice to meet you, M. I'll see you around.

L. See you.

　　　(**PREPPY GIRL** *runs off.*)

(L stays, breathing in the Quad.)
(Inhale. Exhale. A moment of peace. Then –)
(A caw from above.)
(She looks up.)

End of Play

Printed in the USA
CPSIA information can be obtained
at www.ICGtesting.com
LVHW020017280923
759269LV00015B/1075

9 780573 705878